The SIXTEEN HAND Horse

written and illustrated by
FRED GWYNNE

Simon and Schuster Books for Young Readers
Published by Simon & Schuster Inc., New York

Simon and Schuster Books for Young Readers
Simon & Schuster Building
Rockefeller Center
1230 Avenue of the Americas
New York, New York 10020
Copyright © 1980 by Fred Gwynne
Published by the Simon & Schuster Juvenile Division
SIMON AND SCHUSTER BOOKS FOR YOUNG READERS is a
trademark of Simon & Schuster Inc.
Manufactured in the United States of America

10 9 8 7 6 5 4 3   10 9 8 7 6 5 4 3   (pbk)

ISBN 0-671-66291-0   0-671-66968-0 Pbk.

for D.F.G.

Mommy says that she wants a horse that is sixteen hands.

Mommy says

puppies should be
paper trained.

Mommy says that
churches have cannons…

...and bells

that peel.

Daddy   knows a man

who fought a suit and lost.

Daddy says Uncle Arthur

runs a plant...

And they live in an eary house.

Mommy says she and Daddy went to the opera and

were moved by the orchestra.

And sat in a tear.

Daddy says he caught
a fish on a spoon.

Mommy says
    her nose is running.

Daddy says his car
has a crack in its block.

It says on the radio to

watch out for a rabbit dog.

Daddy says there are locks

big enough to hold a battleship.

Daddy says he won't

join the tennis club, because
all the members are wasps.

Daddy says once he knew
        a soldier who was

a wall.

Mommy asked the grocer

to see his fish row.

Daddy says he's going to bank

the fire.

Daddy says he won't play cards

if the steaks are too high.

Daddy says a hunting dog can flush a pheasant.

If you ask me, it's all pigeon English!